The Planet Mars
and Its Inhabitants

Eros Urides

DODO PRESS

THE PLANET MARS AND ITS INHABITANTS

BY EROS URIDES (A MARTIAN)

DEDICATION

To the millions of God's children on this earth enthralled in darkness, for whom the solicitude of the Father is now in evidence, this book is dedicated.

May it be a beacon to light the way of
weary searchers after TRUTH.

CONTENTS

Chapter I. -EROS URIDES, of the City of Urid, planet Mars, the Author, introduces himself and his book THE PLANET MARS AND ITS INHABITANTS.

Chapter II. -He describes the Population Centers, Temperatures and Climate. The whole Planet is gridironed with Canals. (See Diagram.)

Chapter III. -He gives a full description of the marvelous Martian Canal System.

Chapter IV. -Planetary Economy. No Worries, and the Wants of all are supplied by the Commonwealth.

Chapter V. -Property and Property Rights. God, the Creator of it, is considered the Owner of all Property. Material things to the Martians are but Expedients. The Millions of Martians live as one great family, though divided into families. And it is this solidarity and filial consideration towards each other that made the stupendous Canal and other Works possible.

Chapter VI. -Trade and Barter are unknown. Transportation is by Flying Ships, and Gravitational Pull has been overcome. Also, they use Cosmic or Universal Energy. All Distribution is from immense Warehouses.

Chapter VII. -A great many Clairvoyant Visions were seen by the Shorthand Recorder, which make most interesting reading.

Chapter VIII. -Knowledge of God comes from within. Selfishness has been eliminated; and the Martians require no Policemen, Watchmen or other Guardians of the Peace. Christ is known to the Martians as one of the great Powers in the Universe.

Chapter IX. -Mars has no Political System; yet it is controlled by the very Acme of System. Each Individual of their vast population is guided by "The Light Within" and by "LOVE."

Chapter X. -Mars is ruled by LOVE, their only law. There is no Evil, for all are Good; all are Equal. Truth is simple. The people of Mars are ready to stimulate the living of the Christ-Life on other Planets. (This is a wonderful and most Inspiring chapter.)

Chapter XI. -Education and Training of the Individual. They have a Spoken and a Written Language; but Telepathy is often used. Set Rules of Discipline are not required. There are References to Jupiter, Neptune, Uranus, Venus, Mercury, and the two Moons of Mars.

Chapter XII. -Education and Training of the Individual (contd). Vocational Determination. School Age. Marriage. Science and Domestic Science. Relativity of Time, Space, Motion and Matter. All in the whole Universe is ETERNAL MOTION.

Chapter XIII. -Music is an Expression of the Father. "All around us is a beautiful RAINBOW UNIVERSE". About Music of the Spheres, and that Singing is highly developed.

Chapter XIV. -Aeronautics. Inhabited Planets. Sectarianism. No Sound, no Discordant Vibrations disturb the Atmosphere of Mars.

Chapter XV. -Life is an Attribute of the entire Universe. The Planet Jupiter is enveloped in deep gloom and Darkness. Gives much information. Vesta, an Asteroid, is about 500 miles in diameter. Says that communications between Planets of our Solar System and our Earth will soon be realized, and that the initial Message will be from Mars. It will herald a New Era for the people of Earth, and will break down our narrow-minded Theology.

Chapter XVI. -The Risen Christ. All the Mars people have lived on other Planets before, except your Earth. On Mars they live the Christ-Life every day. 10,000 years ago the Mars people accepted Christ as their Savior WITHOUT MURDER.

Chapter XVII. -Physical Environment is the result of Spiritual Causes, and is the Result of our Mental Attitude.

Chapter XVIII. -Material Life is a Lesson, and is necessary for the unfolding of Character. The Martians have mastered their Natural Passions.

Chapter XIX. -Eros gives a graphic Description of a Martian Home and Surroundings, then shows how the Food is manipulated. It is brought from a Central Depot in a Mechanical Contrivance which is run underground, thence up into the Dining room. The Soiled Dishes are run down and off the same way. No Drudgery for the Housewife!

Chapter XX. -"ART. " The Martians have beautiful productions in Painting, Sculpture and Tapestries, some of which depict the Scenes and Episodes incident on Christ's Visit to Mars ten thousand years ago.

Chapter XXI. -Eros Urides has a good deal to write on the subject of "Scientific Sophistry, " which has mostly to do with our Earth.

FOREWORD

It was Eros Urides, the real Martian behind the scenes, who dictated the contents of this book through the medium to Mr. Kennon. It was further stated that "The medium was held in trance for short periods only, as the medium must necessarily experience the atmosphere of Mars which is more rarified than that of your Earth. " Writes also that the medium seemed to have some difficulty, and at first pain in breathing while in the trance condition.

Mr. Kennon also wrote in his foreword of the original book that it was not until January 4, 1920, it was decided to write the book in which the Planet Mars, its people, its form of government, its Art, Industries, Philosophy of life, etc. would for the first time in the history of this world be given.

It appears that Jesus the Christed One of God visited the planets of our Solar system, the planet Mars being one of those visited and investigated. And, as a proof of this it was Jesus Christ who functioned as chairman or presidentat the great Peace Conference held in the vast coliseum on the first sphere of the Heavens of our Earth. That was in the year 1912, as fully reported in "World of Tomorrow, " page 98. It was at that conference He stated that Universal Peace must be speeded up, as there were other planets to be investigated: and that the Earth stood in the way and was becoming a menace to neighboring planets.

The Planet Mars and Its Inhabitants

CHAPTER I.

THE PLANET MARS AND ITS INHABITANTS

Years ago, as you measure time, I was an inhabitant of Mars, your sister planet. My name is Eros Urides (the latter signifying "of Urid"). But a physical name is only an incidental in one's life.

In the Spirit world we are given a name in accordance with our spiritual qualities and gifts and the kind of work we do.

I came into material being as the fruit of the sacred union of my parents. It is not necessary to say aught concerning their social status, for on Mars all who unfold into a material expression of the Father are equal. Equal in rank, station, and in possession of the material fruits of earth.

After my education had been completed I was, in accordance with the Martian system of scientifically determining one's rightful vocation, assigned as overseer to a section of one of the main canals supplying water from the North Polar cap to an impounding reservoir near the city of Urid, the place of my birth.

I was in the 36th year (Martian reckoning) of my physical life on the planet when my transition occurred, which event was the result of my inability to observe, one night, warning signals sent out from a central station advising the eve of a tremendous drop in temperature. This occurred in the Martian autumn, and I succumbed to the intense cold. I was not married, so I left no immediate family except my parents, brothers and sisters.

I have come to your Earth to give your inhabitants some idea of the idealistic life lived by your more advanced brothers. I use the term idealistic in a relative way only, for in God's universe the degrees of material progress of His children are infinite in number.

In giving this information to the inhabitants of your world I have been assisted by the spirits of many former wise children of your Earth.

The Planet Mars and Its Inhabitants

The purpose of the information which I am about to impart to your people is mainly to stimulate and hasten into material expression the reign of God's kingdom on your Earth.

Many will reject this information, but it is God's truth nevertheless. But on the other hand, many of God's children now functioning on your planet will accept the statements as true, and they will be helped and encouraged in their hard struggle for material existence. This struggle, unequal as it is, is the result of darkness engendered by the loss of faith in God.

Man's faith in his Creator, in the ages preceding your present era of darkness, was sublime. Man's attitude towards, and his confidence in the promises of God was as the faith of a child to its parents, whom it has always trusted. But selfishness has gained the upper hand, and is now man's master on your Earth. To break the chains now binding man to self is the purpose of God's holy emissaries, who have descended from high spiritual spheres to your Earth to teach and show men the way out of bondage. They will succeed, for Omniscience has commanded it. It is under their direction that I am now contributing my little part in this movement.

I am only too glad to have been able to give the information contained in this book, and I also appreciate the assistance of all those on your Earth plane who so willingly assisted; but of course we are all obeying the Father's command.

As life is an attribute of the entire universe, the material aspect of all God's creations are the same. That is, life on another planet must be thought of as being no different from what experience teaches you.

All inspiration comes from the Father. Hence, the degree of a race's advancement in point of civilization is in proportion to its spiritual enfoldment. Therefore the material aspect of life, which includes God's evolutionary and non-evolutionary creatures, is the same on every habitable globe in limitless space.

In telling the story of Mars you must be prepared to believe that, from a physical point of view, the Martians are just human beings, differing little from the people of your Earth.

The same may be said concerning the activities of life enjoyed by all of God's creatures. Martians work and have their recreations. They enjoy the fruits of their earth just as you do the fruits of yours. They have invented labor-saving machinery, and indulge in a multitude of industrial pursuits, but with this difference: their economic system is such that the life of the Martian is not the struggle for existence you have created on your Earth. On the contrary it is a pleasurable life in which work is as much enjoyed as is recreation. This condition is due to two causes. First, Mars is much farther advanced as a world in its evolutionary career. Second, the Spiritual enfoldment of its inhabitants is proportionately advanced.

As the Divine Plan is universal in its scope the physical characteristics of Mars, compared to your Earth are, in a general way, the same, with the exceptions shown later in this book.

The inhabitants of Mars enjoy a blue sky, mountains, hills, rocks and dells, clouds, beautiful sunsets, and in fact most of the physical phenomena witnessed by the dwellers of your Earth.

The Martians live and have their being just as your people do, but they are surrounded by a different spiritual and a modified physical environment. They take pleasure in music, art and the study of physical science, but with this difference: the spiritual growth and enfoldment of the individual is considered as most important, and all material advancement as only an aid to ultimate ends.

With main points in view the reader can now readily comprehend the real Martian character, although it may be a disappointment to some who have imagined the inhabitants of Mars as physically different from themselves; or perhaps, as semi-spiritual entities, who have possibly been transplanted from other worlds to undergo a sort of probationary life amid a Paradise of beautiful surroundings and things.

CHAPTER II.

POPULATION CENTERS, TEMPERATURE, CLIMATE

Although Mars is little more than half as large as your Earth, its diameter being 4,200 miles, it contains a larger area of habitable land than the latter, its surface area being approximately 212,000,000 square miles as against 51,000,000 miles for your Earth. Hence our globe supports a larger population about 13,160,000,000 people. Your population is in the neighborhood of 1,645,000,000. Your land area is 161,000,000 square miles less than the land area of Mars. This is for the reason that your oceans occupy a vast surface of your Earth, and Mars has no oceans, as these dried up ages ago. Consequently almost the entire surface of our planet (with exception of some small areas covered with swamps, remnants of ancient seas and oceans, and portions of the extreme Northerly and Southerly Polar caps) is utilized by the Martian inhabitants.

Our planet is gridironed with canals, many hundreds of the main ones being observable through your telescopes, and the art of intensive farming is practised by us to a degree of perfection never dreamed of by the dwellers of your Earth.

Our winters, even in the Equatorial regions are severe, the temperatures at times descending to as low as 80 degrees below zero. However, our springs, summers, and autumns are mild and nearly twice as long as your seasons, for the Martian year is 687 days long. We grow and mature many crops of necessary cereals, fruits and vegetables during the spring and summer months, so that want is never felt by our happy people.

Our method of irrigation is somewhat different from that practised in the arid portions of your Earth. We do not, except in a few instances, flood our lands as you do. Owing to the fact that our atmosphere is much lighter than yours, the normal air pressure being only about 8 pounds to the square inch as against 15 pounds on your Earth, evaporation is very rapid, and the dewfall, as a consequence of much moisture being in the air, is very great.

This heavy humidity also tends to prevent radiation of heat, and the temperature at night does not drop exceedingly low, although frost is not uncommon even in summer. As our vegetation is acclimated and adapted to our environment no damage is done to growing crops by reason of these frosts.

The Martians experience no difficulty in living in a rarified atmosphere. Neither have they abnormally developed lungs. God has made ample provision for the comfort of His creatures throughout all of His infinite creations, and we of Mars are not excepted from this Fatherly care and love.

Should an inhabitant of your Earth be suddenly transported to Mars he could live but a few minutes, for the reason that his lungs could not assimilate enough oxygen from our light atmosphere.

Economy is a science with us. Nothing is wasted. Every possible square inch of ground produces food for man or beast. Even the north and south Arctic regions, after their seasonal thaws blossom forth with vegetal growth, as astronomers on your Earth have observed. These regions produce their quota of food by being utilized as pasturage for our cattle. Immense amounts of forage are also gathered for the long Martian winters, when a greater portion of either the north or south hemisphere is covered with a mantle of snow.

The equatorial regions are always pleasant. No severe wind storms are experienced on Mars; neither do we have lightning or other magnetic disturbances such as you experience.

As a corollary to the tranquility of our inhabitants living in peace, Love and harmony, and the truths of God expressed in our everyday living, the climate is equable, the atmosphere clear and beautiful, the sky serene and sapphire-blue: the severest winds but gentle zephyrs wafted towards the equator from the more remote portions of our globe. Cloudy skies are rare and rainstorms few.

There is no lack of God's gifts on Mars. As intensive farming is a necessity on our planet, plant food or fertilizing elements are plentiful. One of the large white circular spots observed by your astronomers, located in a region on Mars named by them Elysium, and which has been a puzzle to all observers, is an immense deposit of fertilizing chemicals. An immense well is located in this particular spot which gushes forth a never-ending saline solution, highly impregnated with sodium nitrate, potash and other salts. The country for many miles around is covered with a white precipitate which has been carried by the moist air and deposited on the Martian earth. These chemical compounds are refined and used to replenish the soil with plant food.

There are 153,000 centers of population on Mars, but these centers are not congested cities similar to those on your Earth. Every individual has plenty of room to thrive and develop the best within him.

Our cities are not crowded and our buildings are beautiful in their simplicity: large and roomy, with an abundance of sunlight and ample ventilation. White marble and metals are employed for building purposes.

The inhabitants congregate in centers and, owing to our more perfect methods of transportation, go forth daily to their tasks in field or factory, to return at the end of their allotted period to home and fireside.

CHAPTER III.

THE MARTIAN CANAL SYSTEM

The Canal system on Mars is comparatively new. The idea of constructing a planetary Canal system had its incipiency at the time of Christ's visit to our planet. The Master warned the people that they must make provision for their future water supply. At that time (10,000 years ago) the water supply was becoming noticeably scarcer as time went on. It was nearly 3,000 years after the Master's mission to Mars had been concluded that actual construction of the Planetary Canal system was undertaken; and during the intervening 7,000 years and up to the present time, construction on the public waterways has continued.

At the present day the system is most complete, but constant work is required to keep the canals in working order. In addition to the gigantic Canal system, provision had to be made for suitable reservoirs to impound the water after the seasonal thaws at the poles. To this end immense reservoirs were constructed at most canal intersections. In some instances the reservoirs are established between parallel canals; but in every case smaller canals, or laterals, always intersect at these points.

Many of the canals on Mars are double, as they appear to your astronomers. These double waterways parallel each other at a distance of about 75 miles. The reason for this is that as the Martian population is absolutely dependent upon the Polar waters to irrigate their crops, any accident to a canal, such as a land-slide stopping the regular flow of water or the breaking of a lock or gate, would mean a very serious calamity to a great number of people. And for that reason, soon after the main canals were constructed, second and parallel waterways were made for the purpose of guaranteeing an uninterrupted flow of water from the Poles to the Equatorial regions. The result of this was that on many occasions the foresight of the Martian engineers who had the water supply of the planet in charge, saved immense areas from drought.

The rainfall on Mars is almost nil and the immense population (eight times larger than that of your Earth) is entirely dependent on the water supply from the melting Polar caps. Water on Mars is a most precious fluid and there is none to waste. Our oceans evaporated ages ago, and outside of the precipitation of moisture at the poles in the form of snow, none is to be had anywhere else on the planet except in very meager quantities.

The astronomer Lowell of your Earth, who made a life study of our planet, called these reservoirs "Oases, " but he was mistaken in his theory. He concluded that these points, which appear as round disks in the telescope, were centers of population. This conclusion is erroneous. The centers of population on Mars are scattered over the entire planet regardless of the position of the so-called "Oases. " It is quite true that owing to the rapid evaporation of water in the comparatively thin atmosphere of Mars, the dewfall for quite a radius from the center of the reservoirs is considerable, with the result that vegetation springs up, giving the "Oases" the appearance of a diameter of about 75 miles. The reservoirs are about 60 miles across and hold millions of gallons of water.

The same explanation may be given of the Canals. The dewfall on each side is extensive, and the vegetal growth which extends the full length of the water-ways and for thousands of miles in some cases, is most prolific.

The water in the canals, in most instances, is distributed by gravity; but recourse is had to a lock system and to immense pumps for raising the water to proper levels.

The gates of the lock system and the pumps are operated by electricity, the control of which energy is well understood by us. In fact, we are centuries ahead of your Earth people in the knowledge of the use of Electro-magnetic energy. (More will be given on the subject of Electricity in a later chapter.)

Another source of mystery to your astronomers has been the appearance of triangular dark spots at the origin of some of the Martian canals. These have been referred to by your astronomer Lowell as "Carets, " named so by reason of their peculiar shape. These so-called "Carets" are the thoughtful provision for the impounding of a season's supply of water. In other words they are in part a lock system for raising water to the level of some of the main canals, and embrace also a prodigious pumping system.

These so-called "Carets, " as the telescope will show, are located at the edge of some of what appear to you as very dark areas on our planet. These dark areas are Mars' old sea bottoms, and in many instances have been utilized by our engineers as natural reservoirs for water. Their convenient location near the Poles has provided ideal facilities for the preservation of an adequate supply of water.

The construction of Mars' gigantic Canal system, planetary in its extent, might seem to your Earth people an impossible task. And it might prove so to your Earth dwellers should you undertake a similar project in the ages to come when your seas dry up, though it must be remembered that gravity on Mars, compared with your Earth, is as 38 to 100. Excavations of large waterways then becomes a comparatively easy task. We have no high mountains on Mars; in fact, none exceeding 3,000 feet in altitude.

Owing to the difference in gravity the angle of repose on Mars is nearly acute as against 45 degrees on your Earth, which permits of almost perpendicular walls to the canals and lessens the danger of landslides and cave-ins. But above all, the biggest advantage enjoyed by us in the construction of large public enterprises, such as are embraced by our Canal system, is the solidarity and unity of purpose on the part of the Martian people. As Love rules our planet no internal dissension or public misunderstanding exists among its people to retard any undertaking that is necessary for the good of all.

It is lamentable that the dwellers on your Earth are divided against one another. Not only are your false ideals of racial, sociological and religious distinctions a bar to your Spiritual and material progress, but your political and economic falsities are as millstones around your necks, which will ultimately lead you to destruction unless you, as a people, retrace your steps and go back to the pathway pointed out by Christ the Master 2,000 years ago, when He came to your Earth with a message from the Most High. The pathway is LOVE which leads to a true understanding of God and the Kingdom referred to by Christ.

The Martian canals, as telescopic observation will prove in almost all cases, follow straight lines. When necessary, mountains have been cut through down to a proper level. Where the canals cross depressions or old sea-bottoms, immense aqueducts have been constructed of solid stone and concrete in such a manner that the water, in most cases, flows to its destination by gravity.

The Planet Mars and Its Inhabitants

That this has been a stupendous task may be more readily imagined when it is known that the width of the main canals averages from one to twenty miles. This announcement might seem to many unreasonable, but it must be remembered that the volume of water distributed over 212,000,000 square miles of territory is immense. You might ask where this large volume of water comes from.

The POLAR CAPS! During the Martian winter these extend down nearly to the equator, and cover about five-sevenths of the planet's surface when at maximum; and as the snowfall averages from six inches at the edge of the caps to 50 feet at and near the actual Poles, some idea may be gained of the amount of moisture taken care of by these artificial waterways. Ten feet of snow will make 12 inches of water, so there exists on Mars an ample supply for all purposes.

(NOTE—The question as to why many of the canals germinate has been a perplexing one to our astronomers. Lowell observed that many of the main canals germinated a short time after the commencement of the Martian summer, and for a time it was thought that the phenomena might be an optical illusion, and the latter theory was considered seriously by some observers until the double canals were actually photographed at the Flagstaff observatory, but the cause of the doubling was never solved until the receipt of these revelations.)

CHAPTER IV.

PLANETARY ECONOMY

Economy is a virtue long cultivated on the Planet Mars. On your Earth you waste more than you use, not only in food but in the fruits of the Earth. You are using up your resources at a tremendous rate, and some day you must pay the penalty. Witness the wanton destruction of your beautiful forests, the depletion of your coal beds and crude oil deposits. All this waste is the result of lack of Spiritual guidance; a gross materialism: an inordinate selfish greed. Instead of laying up Spiritual treasures you are worshiping at the altar of Mamon. Ultimately you will find your hoardings nothing but tarnished brass—an illusion leading you on to Spiritual destruction.

With the Martians the incentive to live is to express life and be in harmony with the Creator, to develop spiritually and build for Eternity. On Mars each one strives to live for his brother to the end that all may inherit the promised Kingdom when yet as a physical being. Commercialism with us is unknown, for no one works for profit. The products of the toil of all the inhabitants are for the public larder and other necessities and even luxuries.

As a result of this system of public economy and industrialism, sweat-shops, child labor, poor houses, public reformatories, and the long list of pernicious and iniquitous customs in vogue on your Earth are unknown on our planet.

No worries mar the life of the people of Mars. Worry has no place in the Martian mind. The wants of all are supplied by the Commonwealth, and each one contributes his best efforts to the common good, and in return each individual is supplied his every want. This is in accordance with Christ's message: "Seek ye first the Kingdom of God and His righteousness, and all these things shall be added unto you."

CHAPTER V.

PROPERTY AND PROPERTY RIGHTS

On Mars all property is considered as belonging to God, its Creator, who provided it for the enfoldment and comfort of His creatures. No individual lays claim to property in the sense that you Earth dwellers do.

Through God's love does man inhabit a portion of the material universe, but only for a season. Man comes into material being to express life and acquire an individuality, after which he passes out of material bondage, when his place is taken by another.

At man's transition he takes with him only character, nothing else. If the things he has striven for during his material life have been but chimeras: the material things of life: the fruits of the Earth, then in that case he will find himself poor indeed. The only real wealth, the only thing worth striving for, is a knowledge of God and His Kingdom. And with us Martians a knowledge of God is the ultimate goal sought for. Hence all material things to the Martian are but expedients, soon to be forgotten.

Material wealth is an abstraction. Its usual evidence is the possession of property, which may be money, land, goods or chattels, as the case may be. In final analysis this concrete evidence of wealth is not real.

Money is nothing more or less than a stamped token entitling the possessor to so much human effort, for the real value behind money, after all, is but so much human energy or force, varying according to its quality and its worth.

Other forms of property such as goods and chattels, are the result of human endeavor and may be secured by the exchange of money, or it may be produced by the owner.

Wealth represented by lands, which were created by God for the benefit of all humankind. and not for the individual, is the so-called right-secured by barter, exchange or inheritance, to use or withhold from use, at the caprice of the owner—of a certain piece or portion of the planet. Under a legal fiction the title to land extends to the center of the Earth and to infinity in an opposite direction!

The text: "Thou shalt earn thy bread by the sweat of thy brow" has a deep significance to one who has come into a knowledge of Truth. Drones have no place in the Divine Plan. It is not only essential but mandatory, that each one do his part for the common good. The non-producing rich man is as much a drone as is the vagabond who neither toils nor spins. The Biblical test concerning the difficulty of the rich man getting into Heaven means that it is impossible for a drone or parasite to get into harmony with God.

The possession of wealth is not in itself sinful, but the possession of wealth is a corollary to selfishness. He who is unselfish will spurn wealth. The individual who accumulates beyond his needs sins against Heaven when he locks up his goods in strong boxes. The act of hoarding deprives some creature of his just portion, for God has planned there should be sufficient for all who make the effort, and a system that permits an unequal distribution of God's gifts is in opposition to the Divine Plan, and doubly pernicious is a church organization that permits it.

Only after Christ has taken up His abode in the hearts of the people of your Earth will surcease come to the suffering millions on your planet.

Happiness and selfishness are so diametrically opposed that the former is impossible unless the latter is eliminated from your world, for only real happiness comes after complete surrender to God. Surrender to God means subordination to His will. His will on Earth must be done as it is in Heaven. All must be self-conscious of this. If God's will was adhered to on your Earth what a different place it would be! Instead of a shambles it would be a paradise, the brotherhood of man and the Fatherhood of God a fact instead of the dream of a few.

God loves all His creatures, both evolutionary and non-evolutionary. His love is infinite in extent. We are all His children. Everything has been provided for us. It is only man's selfishness that deprives any creature of his just dues. Man suffers want on account of his lack of faith in God! Before man lost his faith in God he walked and communed with angels. He could do it now if he would but listen to the Voice Within—if he would only open his heart to Christ, for help is ready whenever one asks for it in sincerity and faith.

One of the sources of great injustice to the majority of the inhabitants of your Earth is the belief in the dogma of Divine Right. This dogma includes not only the absurdity of the Divine Right of kings, but the Divine Right to the ownership of goods and land through the Creator's favoritism for a few.

This dogma is the mother of untold misery and suffering. Out of this ungodly theory has evolved your shameful caste system; your shameful economic ideas.

Your ancient feudal system of government has been but little improved upon today over its primitive status, for you still draw well-defined lines of class distinction between God's children—lines of demarcation based on wealth and natal origin. With your inhabitants, communal standing and social distinction is proportionate to the wealth of the possessor or to the wealth or social standing of ancestors.

The monstrous heresy of Divine Right is an invention of the powers of darkness and must be eliminated from your world root and branch before your progress forward is assured. God plays no favorites. His love is showered upon all alike. His gifts are for all His children. It was never the Divine intent that a favored few should bask in the sunshine of His grace while the majority suffered want and deprivation. These false ideas have been the procurers of darkness: of the Stygian gloom now overshadowing your Earth.

Spiritual darkness has not always covered your Earth. In primitive times—ages ago—eras whose history has been lost to you, man on your Earth was in harmony with his Creator. This was in the Golden Age when man and the angels of God walked hand in hand; when man communed with God, and when the Christ spirit was abiding in the hearts of the people. In this age man was spiritually developed to a degree almost unbelievable by you.

Then the time came when man listened to the temptor (his baser self), and through the workings of the law of Atavism man degenerated almost to the level of his animal prototype.

This incident in your world's history is the source of the legend of the "Fall of Man" in the "Garden of Eden. " Man disobeyed God by listening to self, by giving himself over to his selfish desires. He slew his brother, figuratively speaking, when he abandoned himself to selfish ends and took advantage of his fellowman. He has been guilty of that sin ever since. IT IS NOW INHERENT IN HIS MAKE-UP; THIS SELFISH INSTINCT MUST BE ELIMINATED BEFORE HE CAN AGAIN FIND THE FATHER'S KINGDOM.

No fences or other evidences of individual ownership surround the millions of homes on Mars. No lines of demarcation divide one plot of land from another. The millions of beautiful homes—beautiful in their simplicity, for over-ornamentation such as the dwellers of your Earth practise, is not tolerated on our planet—belong to the Commonwealth. The same are allotted to the individual as a life tenure only.

The same custom prevails in the matter of personal property. Should a Martian have use for a flying machine, also used by another, or other kind of property for personal use, he does not ask the use of same in the spirit that your Earth dwellers borrow from one another. Use of the needed article is requested with the idea that it belongs to the community: that all material possessions are the common property of the entire race.

THE MILLIONS OF MARTIANS LIVE AS ONE FAMILY. IT IS THIS SOLIDARITY, THIS FILIAL CONSIDERATION THAT ONE HOLDS FOR THE OTHER THAT HAS MADE THE STUPENDOUS AND GIGANTIC PUBLIC WORKS ON MARS POSSIBLE.

In the absence of a universal unity of purpose intelligent life on Mars would have become extinct centuries ago, when the last remnants of its oceans and seas dried up and a planetary irrigation system became necessary in order to utilize the frozen Polar moisture.

The Planet Mars and Its Inhabitants

CHAPTER VI.

DISTRIBUTION OF COMMODITIES

Barter and trade are unknown on Mars. The entire race of Martians is cooperative, and the production of all necessities is based on the needs of the Commonwealth.

Specialization in different branches of industrial activity is centralized, as is the case of your Earth. That is, some particular parts of the planet, owing to climatic and other conditions, are better adapted for the production of some special kind of raw material used in the manufacture of clothes or other necessities of life, or the production of some particular foodstuff. But in every case the incentive for industrial activity is not material profit. On the contrary the real incentive is compliance with the Father's will.

Transportation is effected by means of flying ships actuated by the control of gravitational attraction. These vehicles of the air, beside your crude affairs[1] are most perfect, and the amount of freight carried is unlimited, for the reason that the gravitational attraction of the cargo is nullified as well as that of the ship. (A more extended explanation concerning this matter is given in another section of this book.) Another motive power used is Cosmic, or Universal Energy. (We shall refer to this later.)

[1] NOTE — Yes, 35 years ago, but not today, 1955.

Immense warehouses and depots are scattered throughout the entire planet. These are centers of distribution. These warehouses are filled with what all the people of the entire planet need in the way of food, clothing and other necessities of life. These depots are in charge of trained and competent workers who attend to the issuance and distribution of all commodities.

When a Martian is in need of any particular commodity he makes application to have his want supplied to the depot nearest to his habitation. He immediately receives the needed article. If the quantity and nature of his requisition is too large for him to carry personally, the same is delivered at his domicile by the Commonwealth's Transportation Department.

The Planet Mars and Its Inhabitants

CHAPTER VII.

CLAIRVOYANT VISIONS OF MARS

In connection with the revelation contained in this book concerning the physical characteristics of Mars, the compiler of this volume, as well also as the medium, was given much information concerning this advanced planet by means of clairvoyant visions. These pictures were given the writer at different times, commencing early in 1920, and continuing until the book was finished.

As has been explained by the controls who have been instrumental in giving the information about Mars, the purpose of these clairvoyant pictures was to give the compiler of this book real visual evidence as to life on Mars; and in particular, real pictures setting forth its topography, which could be elucidated in no other way.

Written descriptions of scenery and of human activities necessarily fall short of the reality, especially when an attempt is made to record a series of events or a point of view outside the realm of our experience.

The first picture realized by the writer, and for that matter the most important one, was the view given him of Urid the Beautiful, one of the most Important centers of population on the planet Mars.

It was while lying in bed one morning the writer was contemplating the many messages being received from the Martian, who is the dictator of the subject matter of this book, that he found himself at a strange place, suspended as it were in the air over a beautiful lake of blue water, whose surface was broken by gentle ripples, due to the soft, balmy breeze blowing over the surface of the water. The writer was facing what seemed to be a westerly direction; and at a distance of about five miles there arose a series of small mountains about 2,500 feet in altitude. These mountains skirted the shores of the lake. The sky was a beautiful blue, bluer than the sapphire-tinted skies of our own desert lands. The mountains were tinted red from base to top, except where the moisture near the shores of the lake had stimulated a vegetal growth, whose green contrasted most harmoniously with the red of the soil. Two white clouds floated majestically near the peaks of the highest mountains.

The Planet Mars and Its Inhabitants

The atmosphere was impressively clear and all objects seemed to stand out in sharp definition, a condition seldom seen by dwellers on our Earth except in extremely dry and arid regions.

On top of a small plateau, forming the crown of a low-lying hill at the base of one of the highest mountains, and about 1,500 feet from the shore line, I was startled to see a large city. The thousands of closely nestling buildings seemed to be built of white stone. The writer was lost in admiration, for there in front of him the pure white of the city, contrasting so vividly with the red soil of this faraway planet, stood the habitations of an advanced race many millions of miles removed from my own world.

The writer was impressed with the fact that, with but few exceptions, the buildings of gleaming white were all one story in height, and it became instantly evident that crowding is not tolerated by the inhabitants of this progressive planet. A few structures towered above the rest. These, as the writer was informed later, were the public buildings dedicated to the use of the people as lecture halls, centers for music and art, etc.

On a subsequent occasion the writer was shown a close-up view of Urid. Flowers, grass and green foliage abounded everywhere. The long streets were broad and well paved, and flanked on two sides with long rows of one-storied buildings of white stone, beautiful in their simplicity. No extreme ornamentation is carried out in the erection of buildings on Mars. On the contrary, the simple square outlines characteristic of our own Old Mission architecture seems to prevail on the planet Mars. The same simple style prevails with the public buildings, except that massive stone columns marked the portals of same, reminding one of our own early Grecian architecture.

Many palm-like trees grew all over the city, especially in the neighborhood of the public buildings.

A week after the occurrence of the above incident the writer was shown, in the same manner as before, one of the many canals that gridiron the Martian globe. This particular canal is one of the main waterways on Mars, and appeared to be about a mile wide at the point of observation. The water was of a deep blue color, denoting great depth. Along the banks of this waterway could be seen many houseboats or floating dwellings. Some of these houseboats were very large and evidently housed large families. The writer was informed that many Martians who have charge of the waterways dwell in these habitations.

The banks above the canal were covered with green grass and many flowers.

On subsequent occasions I was shown other canals and reservoirs, and the manner in which some of the canals were cut through the mountains. In some instances the walls of the canals were almost perpendicular. Steep cuts, even in soft ground, seemed to be characteristic of all the waterways observed by the writer.

On another occasion the writer was given a view of the North Polar regions. At that time the deep snows that covered the ground everywhere were melting. The country seemed to be very hilly. As far as the eye could reach I observed low-lying hills covered with a white mantle of snow. Patches of reddish earth here and there indicated that the thaw was general and that the snow had thinned out in spots. Between the hills I observed a large body of water, and was informed that this was an artificial reservoir which had been created by the damming of a large valley. The sky on this occasion was hidden by a mist, a very natural phenomenon in view of the fact that many thousands of square miles of the country, covered with snow on this part of Mars, was undergoing a rapid thaw.

That the large dark-colored areas on Mars, supposed by early observers to be seas, are nothing more or less than low, swampy land covered with rank vegetation, was evidenced to me on one occasion when I was permitted to see the true character of these portions of the planet.

The rank vegetation was about three feet high and of a greenish red color. Interspersed throughout the mass of coarse-leafed plants were high, dry stalks the remnants of an earlier crop of Martian flora. The season seemed to be advanced and all plant life was taking on autumnal tints.

It was in December 1919 that I saw the first close-up picture of a Martian—a woman. Her head was covered with a thin veil which came down to her well-formed mouth. She seemed to be a most beautiful woman with most expressive eyes. Her hair was black. Her skin was unusually white, which contrasted with the dark hair. She wore no jewelry, or other ornaments that I could see.

On a subsequent occasion I was permitted to see a Martian male. He was playing a flutelike instrument, and as he was quite close to me I could observe the wax-like texture of his skin. This semi-transparency of the skin is characteristic of the Martians, and evidences a life that is free from the many bodily ailments that afflict humanity on our Earth. The Martian was dressed in graceful but loose-fitting clothes of a reddish-brown color. His eyes were a deep blue and his lips seemed to be unusually red. In respect to stature he was, I would say, about five feet nine inches in height. In fact, on subsequent occasions I have observed crowds of Martians gathered together and they appeared no different from the inhabitants of our own world except as to clothing, which is much simpler, but more graceful than our styles.

I was informed by the spiritual control that the fauna of Mars is varied, but that all animal life is domesticated, there being now no wild animals on the planet.

It was shortly after I had seen the Martians, described in the foregoing paragraph, that I was shown two cat-like animals, which at the time of my vision were engaged in playing about the feet of a Martian. They did not exactly resemble cats, but were more feline than canine. They were about the size of a large Airedale, and of a dark, reddish-brown color with deep black stripes, similar to the markings of our tigers. They were very playful and cavorted about just as our own dogs and cats do when endeavoring to attract the attention of their masters.

On the morning of January 20, 1920, I was shown another Martian canal. On this occasion I observed a large building on the banks of the waterway near my point of vision. This building was more of a grandstand with a roof than anything else I can compare it to. It consisted of a large framework painted white, and was as high as our two-storied structures. A multitude of the people were inside the building, some sitting, some standing. They all seemed to be intently gazing in a Northerly direction, up-stream.

Much green foliage and varied-colored flowers lined the banks of the canal, especially in the neighborhood of the building. The people all

The Planet Mars and Its Inhabitants

seemed to be attired in holiday garb, and it was evident to me that a celebration was going on.

Later I was informed that what I had witnessed was an annual celebration observed by the people of Mars on the occasion of arrival of the first water from the North Pole after commencement of the Martian Spring. It appears that this occasion is a very important event with the Martians. as the arrival of the life- giving moisture from the Arctic and Antarctic regions of the planet insures a season of plenty for the inhabitants. The water arrives at the equatorial regions in a little less than a Martian month (60 days) after the commencement of the Polar thaws and after a season of thanksgiving to the Father has been held by all in appreciation of His bountiful gifts. The Spiritual leaders of the different communities preside at these gatherings.

The foregoing is in remarkable agreement with a statement on page 375 of the late Professor Lowell's book titled "MARS, " as follows.

"The Canal quickening on Mars occupied 52 days, as evidenced by the successive vegetal darkenings which descend from latitude 72 degrees North and latitude 0, a journey of 2,650 miles. The rate of progression is remarkably uniform, and this fact that it is carried from near the Pole to the Equator is sufficient tell-tale of extrinsic aid, and the uniformity of the action increases its significance. "

On the morning of January 21 I witnessed another interesting Martian scene, which was almost identical with the previous vision of the Arctic regions of this planet, except that the warm season was more advanced, and I was permitted to see the country from another angle. I was facing East. Most of the Polar snow had disappeared, and the low-lying hills were now covered with a growth of dark green vegetation, except at a few isolated points which showed small patches of snow. The sky was less misty than on the previous occasion.

On the evening of January 21 I was shown a flock of Martian sheep. The herd was small and I observed five of the animals at close range. I call them sheep for the reason that the animals resembled our sheep in every particular. The wool was very long and of a dark reddish-brown color, except underneath their bellies which was yellowish.

The Planet Mars and Its Inhabitants

On the evening of January 29 I had a vision of a beautiful woman with a child kneeling at her feet. She was seated on a chair and held a book on her lap. The symbolism of the vision was later explained to me by the controls. who said: "Verily I say unto you whosoever shall not receive the Kingdom of God as a little child, he shall not enter therein." God's truths are perceived only by those who can acquire the simple faith of a child.

It was about the same time I had a vision in which I saw Sergius for the first time distinctly. He is the principal control dominating the writing of this book. He appeared very patriarchal with a long beard. His features were decidedly semitic. His countenance was most spiritual and beautiful.

On February 10 I had my first vision of Mars' two moons, known to our astronomers as Diemos and Phobos. The latter appeared as a satellite about half as large as our full moon, and the former like a star brighter than the first magnitude, and could be compared with Jupiter as seen from our Earth during a favorable opposition of that planet. The latter satellite sheds considerable light on her primary. An interesting explanation of these two moons will be found in a later chapter of this book.

On February 17 I was shown the actual appearance of our sun from the planet Mars. What I saw disproves the theory that owing to the distance of Mars from the sun the latter would be viewed by the Martians as a disk about half the size as seen from our Earth. The Solar Orb appeared as to size and brightness, about the same as viewed from our Earth, and seemed to give forth its heat with the same intensity. I was facing the sun and its brilliance blinded my eyes for an instant.

On the evening of February 29 I had a vision of a strange looking creature ape-like in appearance. The form was about five feet tall, very hairy, his body being covered with a thick coat of woolly hair of a grayish color. He was smoking what appeared to be a cigar-like roll of something, probably some sort of leaves rolled up into a convenient form for smoking. On the tips of his pointed ears were little tufts of long hair, which gave his head a lynx-like appearance. There were quite a number of large yellow spots on his hairy chest. His nose was very stubby, and his entire face was decidedly apelike.

The Planet Mars and Its Inhabitants

I was later informed that I had seen an inhabitant of the planet Mercury, where life has not yet evolved to a very high degree, and where man has not yet wholly emerged from his primary beast-like state.

Concerning the flora of Mars I have on various occasions viewed orchards of growing fruit trees. The trees were set out in rows similar to the methods adopted in our own orchards. The trees were dwarf-like, being not over five or six feet high. I was informed that this particular species of tree was cultivated for its fruit and for the fiber obtained from its large leaves, which is made into cloth, thread and cordage.

On one occasion a short time after the chapter dealing with the transmission of Electro-magnetic energy by wireless was received, I was shown two immense towers on the planet Mars which are used for the purpose of distributing power throughout the planet. The two towers were very close together, probably 100 yards apart and 100 feet high. They resembled two immense round smoke-stacks, such as are common in our factory districts. The tops of the towers were surmounted by oval caps, transparent as if made from glass, and protected by a system of grill work. While I was intently observing the towers there occurred a blinding flash of light simultaneously from the two oval caps.

The surrounding country was covered with high trees, and it was impossible for me to observe the base of the two structures.

CHAPTER VIII.

KNOWLEDGE OF GOD COMES FROM WITHIN

Mars, with its teeming millions of inhabitants, whose dwellings, factories, storehouses, etc. cover most of the entire area, has no watchmen, policemen or other guardians of the peace to prevent unlawful acts on the part of its people.

As all property is considered as belonging to the Father, and is held in common by the people of the planet, there exists no incentive for anyone to steal. Each individual has all he requires for his comfort. Hence, why should anyone covet what is in the possession of his brother?

There is no temptation on Mars for anyone to take more than he needs, for selfishness has been entirely eliminated from our planet. Selfishness has no place among really civilized beings. It is a relic of the jungle where it is necessary to perpetuate the lower animal life.

You of your Earth have reverted or degenerated to a primordial condition or state through the law of Atavism. This is a part of your fall from Divine Grace. And to induce man on your globe to realize his pitiful condition and redeem himself is the work of the Spirits from the higher Spheres who are now with you.

Mars has no Church system and no Ecclesiastical Hierarchy. All Martians recognize and worship one God, the Eternal Father. Each individual is taught from infancy to seek God through the doors of his own soul, which is an institutional faculty possessed by everyone.

Jesus Christ, who came to your Earth 2,000 years ago with a message, is known to us. The Christ is one of the greatest powers in the Universe—next to the Creator.

Your sectarian church systems are a hindrance to the proper spiritual development of the individual. These systems engender an element of dependability on the individual which holds back his spiritual enfoldment and perverts his true individuality, which must grow and unfold before real progress upwards begins.

The Planet Mars and Its Inhabitants

All knowledge of God should come from within and not through the instrumentality of imperfect individuals, such as your religious teachers are.

The present lack of interest (in 1920) in sectarian matters on the part of the inhabitants of your Earth is evidence of a slow but sure disintegration of a system that has held your people in mental and spiritual bondage for centuries, and presages the dawn of a better day for humanity on your Earth.

CHAPTER IX.

MARS HAS NO POLITICAL SYSTEM

When Love rules a community of people there is no need of administrative bureaus for the regulation of the lives of the inhabitants who make up the population of a planet. For the same reason Mars has no gubernatorial or political administrative center.

This announcement may, in a measure, be a disappointment to many readers who have imagined that no considerable number of human beings could live and prosper without the aid and guidance of a complex administrative system such as you have on your Earth.

Bureaucracy and autocracy are evils resulting from an undeveloped civilization, and have no place in a community where selfishness has been eliminated.

When each individual of a vast population, such as that of Mars, is actuated and guided by the Light Within there is no need for a horde of political parasites to direct the destinies of the race.

This lack of an administrative system on Mars also applies to its industrial and economic side. The law of supply and demand determines just how many factories there should be, and just what output is necessary for a given period. But it must be remembered that the law of supply and demand on our planet has no relation to a competitive system such as yours, for we have no competitor, a fact that will be impressed elsewhere in this book.

It is true that certain of our people who have been specially singled out by the dominating influence of the Invisible World are occasionally appealed to by those in doubt as to what is best for their individual welfare, or the welfare of the community at large, to act in advisory capacities. These are the Spiritual Advisers of the planet, and are really God's prophets. There was a time when your race was guided by similar individuals, as is evidenced from mention of them in your sacred Scriptures. But their usefulness was lost when man on your Earth forgot God.

It was then that man mistrusted the Light Within, and disregarded the unwritten laws graven in the soul by the Creator. He clamored for a Code of Laws and received them (through Moses). His next downward step was taken when he admitted it was necessary to have interpreters of the Law: for if the spirit of the Law had been kept there would have been no misunderstanding or juggling of the letter.

Soon there was so much of this turning and twisting to suit man's growing selfishness, that there was need for someone in authority over all the interpreters, whose word should be final. So your people cried aloud for Kings. And you have them, and your law has grown to immense proportions, as have also the clever sins of your selfishness. WHERE THERE IS NO SIN THERE IS NO NEED OF LAWS; FOR THE RIGHTEOUS MAN IS A LAW UNTO HIMSELF.

It must not be imagined that because of the lack of a political system on Mars, such as you deem necessary on your Earth, that all is chaos and life a sort of happy-go-lucky existence. On the contrary, the Martian existence is controlled by the acme of system, which is in accordance with the law of Divine Harmony. A system from which has been eliminated all the useless wheels which so clog up your lives and make your progress slow indeed.

CHAPTER X.

MARS IS RULED BY LOVE

"And now abideth Faith, Hope and Love: these three; but the greatest of these is LOVE. " Paul to the Corinthians.

THERE IS BUT ONE LAW ON MARS. THAT LAW IS LOVE.

This law is not written in a code for the guidance of the people.

It is graven in the hearts of the inhabitants, and is reflected in the countenance of every individual.

This law is the incentive before the entire population and urges each individual onward to the completion of the task before him.

There are no rulers to bow before: neither is anyone better than his brother. There is no evil, for all are good: all are equal. God endows every individual expression of life with the Divine Heritage of a pure soul. It is the individual's concern to keep this heavenly gift unstained in its descent into matter. The love force of the Spirit is the potent agent that does this for the individual when allowed to permeate and radiate the entire being. When individuals have learned to bathe their innermost beings in the Father's love, then it must follow that a nation made up of such individuals will be governed only by such precepts as are evolved from this dominating Love-force.

It is of no import to the individual on this planet what his particular task may be, for all work is for the Father; and the humblest vocation (humbler from the point of view of the dwellers on your Earth) is as important and as honorable as the highest.

MARS IS RULED BY LOVE, which is in accordance with the Divine Intent. It is the desire of the Father that every world in limitless space inhabited by His children be ruled by that Divine Principle. For when Love is the supreme law of a world, as it is of the Universe, there is no need of a system of complex laws and a horde of judicial officers to interpret and enforce them.

The Planet Mars and Its Inhabitants

When Love enters into the life of a community selfishness makes its exit: misery becomes a stranger and pain and sickness vanish.

From the cradle to transition the Martian is dominated by Love and guided by the Father's will. The result of this Love-rule is individual and communal happiness. But above all, a Spiritual progress that unfolds the individual in accordance with the Cosmic Intent.

To die, in the sense of passing out of one's physical environment, is the destiny of every created being. Hence, in that sense, death exists on Mars as it does on your Earth. But the real death referred to by Christ: a Spiritual death imposed on man by his fall from Grace, a penalty for having forgotten God, is unknown on this planet Mars. We are in harmony with the Father. Those who are spiritually dead are cut off from the Father as a result of their indifference and ignorance of Spiritual Truth.

The religion of the Martian may be expressed in two thoughts: "LOVE" and "THY WILL BE DONE, NOT MINE. " The true definition of Religion is a "RULE OF LIFE, " and as our lives are guided entirely by Love and the Father's Will. WE HAVE A RELIGION.

You, on your Earth, have created a Religion to satisfy your conventionalities. Truth is simple, but you have made it intricate. It is free, yet you buy it from the would-be disciples. Both you and we must approach Him in simple faith: "Unless ye become as little children ye cannot enter the Kingdom of Heaven. "

Speaking of children, I desire to give expression to a thought that may appear to be outside the subject: it is this: The beauty and simplicity of youth is wonderful, and to be admired by all: but in the sight of the Heavenly Father, and those who have progressed to higher realms, it is not so wonderful as those older characters who have waded the marshes of life, as it were, and who have trod the dirty steps without losing faith.

This is to encourage those who sometimes think when they look back on their lives that all is dark. Their strength is being tried in the darkness. Therefore their courage and faith is so much more.

We who are giving you these messages have passed beyond the stage you are in, and do not have to be tried on every hand. We look upon you who are struggling through the pitfalls created by your false systems with pity, knowing how great your trials are. Do not think that because we have gone on to higher planes of life that we are out of sympathy with you. The more we bask in the sunshine of Love the more tender we become to those in the shadow. And if you would only realize how strong you are, with the Father's love and His real consideration for you, you would try so much harder to better your condition by meeting His Love with Love.

We of Mars have learnt to keep the right pictures before the minds of our youth that they may not be so sorely tried, but on your planet you have not even the beginning of a system whereby there could be kept continually before the minds of your children the real goal to be striven for. I make exception of the few homes on your planet where the parents are in spiritual growth, but these homes are not ideal—just a beginning of Idealism. But they are better far than the masses in their home conditions on your planet.

Now, we are ready to do all we can towards stimulating the living of the Christ-life among all souls in the Universe when it can be so arranged: but it will take aeons of time on some planets, and many decades on yours before we can scientifically teach you. To be sure, we are giving you all we can for this book, but it will not be universally accepted, although it will bring great joy to those who have faith.

If you can keep some of the pictures we are giving you of the wonderful happiness we possess it will help you in the sordidness of your own life. Picture beautiful things and your heart must be beautiful. Strive with all your mind to hold beautiful thoughts, for it is well worth your every effort towards faith.

CHAPTER XI.

EDUCATION AND TRAINING OF THE INDIVIDUAL

The people of Mars have a spoken and written language, but not so filled with complexities as yours, for the reason that owing to the high development of the mental faculties thoughts are almost as audible as words. Hence, converse between individuals on our planet is not altogether a series of vocal ejaculations. On the contrary, among the older members of the race, communication between individuals is in some cases audibly imperceptible.

Printed books are used, but mostly for the very young, as information is usually transmitted impressionally.

Education on Mars begins at the mother's knee. The first knowledge imparted to the young is Spiritual. The first lessons given to the child are: One's absolute dependence on God, and that the few years before the individual are but an unfoldment, or an individualizing of the entity into a separate and distinct unit.

The Spiritual lessons are amplified as the child grows and grasps these truths. This procedure continues until the pupil is ready to enter an institution of learning.

THE HOME IS THE PRIMARY SCHOOL, JUST AS A PHYSICAL EXISTENCE ON A PLANET IS THE KINDERGARTEN OF A NEVER-ENDING LIFE. THE PARENTS ARE THE FIRST TEACHERS.

The primary education consists, as already said, in lessons on the necessity of expressing God in our lives in truth and righteousness in order that the mind of the individual be so moulded and fashioned that absolute faith is placed in God's promises through the Master, Christ.

The keynote to the education of the individual is that one must first seek God's Kingdom, and that all knowledge and wisdom, which is the Divine Heritage of all, will be easily attained: and that coming into a knowledge of God means health, happiness and wisdom.

The Planet Mars and Its Inhabitants

After the individual has grasped the primary lessons, which result in an unfoldment of the spirit within, he is then sent to a school; but a school system different from anything you have on your Earth. The task of the teacher is, not to teach knowledge but to assist in bringing out what is already latent in the soul, rather than a set routine, for every individual is considered a master in some line of thought and activity. The pupil is led into knowledge instead of being taught directly.

The individual is left to his own tastes and volition. The harmony of music of God's laws, which embrace Astronomy, Physics and of Life, together with a knowledge of the laws of Electricity, is especially brought to the attention of the individual. You of the Earth know as yet very little concerning the true nature of Electricity. Your methods of handling and generating this wonderful force are crude indeed, by comparison with the deep knowledge attained on Mars with the subject.

And so with the study and development of the Harmony of Music, we of Mars have developed a high spiritual sense, and are able to hear and see many intermediate degrees of vibration that do not exist at all for you. Of course there are some exceptions among the few of your Earth who, after having striven hard for light have been favored by God's angels in the development of a higher Spirituality.

Our teachers are guides who look after their charges in an atmosphere of Love and, as a result, right conceptions of Truth are acquired by the pupil.

Thought is the expression or fruit of the Spirit, and Martian children are never allowed to forget their Spiritual growth. As a consequence of this they are easily led into true knowledge, and having a broad vision are able to see all things in their true relations. They begin at the cause and work towards the effect, which is the opposite of your system.

No set rules of discipline are used in the schools. Indeed they are not necessary for the reason that the one ideal: the one goal impressed on the mind of the pupil is the complete expression of the Father Within, for to express the Father is to have perfect life, life in abundance.

The Planet Mars and Its Inhabitants

Concentration of mind, economy of time and energy are studied and learned by the child in the early part of his career.

Astronomy on our planet offers an ideal field in seeking an understanding of the reign of immutable law through the Infinite Universe of God, and owing to the clear rarified atmosphere of Mars, unusual opportunity is presented to students in visual observations of the Heavens.

Entire classes of advanced students, accompanied by their teacher guides repair to the open at night when the canopy of God's Heavens is ablaze with scintillating points of light. The different constellations as viewed from our planet present the same general appearance as to configuration as they do to the dwellers on your Earth; but the view is decidedly more vivid by reason of a more advantageous viewpoint.

The so-called Superior planets, such as Saturn, Jupiter, some of the larger asteroids, and Uranus and Neptune, are nearer to Mars than to Earth, and for that reason are more easily discerned from this vantage point. Some of the satellites of Jupiter are easily seen with the naked eye.

Your Earth appears to us about as Jupiter does to you, and with our observing instruments we are able to see your continent and oceans when not covered by a cloud canopy.

As to the so-called Inferior planets Venus and Mercury, the former presents the appearance of a star of the first magnitude, but being so near the sun it is only visible an hour before or after sunset, depending upon its position. But Mercury, being so near the Solar Orb, it is rarely its position is favorable for observation from our planet, and then only with our more perfect telescopes.

Our students view the phenomena of eclipses of the sun and our planet with the greatest interest, just as your astronomers do.

Mars' two moons present what would appear to you a most striking phenomenon, for one rises in the East and the other in the West, passing each other at times within view of observers. The most distant satellite of Mars is known to us as Laster, to which has been given the name of Deimos by the first observers on your Earth. Approximately 132 hours elapse between its rising and setting at any particular point on our planet, as a consequence of the fact that it revolves in 30 hours 18 minutes at a distance of 14,600 miles more or less from its primary; and as Mars rotates in 24 hours 37 minutes from East to West the motion is almost neutralized by the circulation of this satellite.

During the time of its rotation it changes four times from full to new and new to full. The appearance of this satellite to the Martians is equal, if not a little brighter than the view of Jupiter from your Earth.

The second satellite, known to us as Benii, and to your astronomers as Phobos, sheds considerable amount of light on the Martian landscape by means of its large size and close proximity, being distant about 3,700 miles from the surface of Mars. This satellite is shut out from view beyond 69 degrees latitude by reason of the curvature of its primary. Its period is 7 hours and 30 minutes — less than one-third the time of the rotation of Mars. It rises in the West and courses across the Heavens in 11 hours, during which time it undergoes one entire cycle of its phases and gets through half another. Its disc appears to us as a little more than half of the moon's disc on your Earth at full appears to you.

The realm of Physics presents another interesting study to the Martian student. We have advanced to the study of Nature's laws to a point which would appear to your understanding most incomprehensible. Long ago we mastered the knowledge of the method of releasing Interatomic Energy, [2] a knowledge which in the brain of an unscrupulous person would be most disastrous, not only to himself but to those about him. The energy locked up in an atom of matter is tremendous, and the release of this power is only a matter of knowing the law. The inhabitants of your world will have to bide a long time before the key that will release this giant is placed within their reach.

[2] The Popular Science Monthly, May, 1920, printed the following — "Sir Oliver Lodge thinks that man is not yet civilized enough to use the energy hidden in ordinary matter. The time will come when atomic energy will take the place of coal as a source of power. " The man who spoke thus before the Royal Society of Arts in London was Sir Oliver Lodge — one of the towering figures in modern science, a man who has devoted the better part of his life to the study and interpretation of the atom. This new form of energy, which our great-grandchildren may utilize instead of oil and coal, has

possibilities so appalling that Sir Oliver almost rejoices that we do not know how to release it. I hope that the human race will not discover how to use this energy, he says, until it has brains and morality enough to use it properly, because if the discovery is made by the wrong people this planet would be unsafe. A force utterly disproportionate to the present source of Power would be placed at the disposal Or the world."

NOTE (By the Editor in 1920) — This article was published more than two months after the revelation above was received, but is another striking confirmation of the truth of these revelations.

Not until you have eliminated your inherent selfishness; not before you have learnt the lesson as Christ taught it will you be permitted to harness one of the mightiest forces in the universe, a force equally as great for evil as it is for good. This knowledge we have, and we have utilized it in the construction and building of our mighty planetary projects.

This Interatomic Energy is the source of the sun's continuous heat. If it were combustion the Solar orb would have burnt itself out ages ago. All your theories to account for the continuity of solar radiation are in error. The release of Interatomic Energy in the sun at a definite rate is the reason why its heat never increases or diminishes though millions of years come and go in endless procession.

And this process is not the working of a blind, senseless force, some of your scientists would have you believe, but the Creator: Omnipotent, Omniscient, Omnipresent is the Dominator: the Directing Intelligence, who sees to it that all is provided for His children.

On your Earth you have thus far discovered some 85 elements. In order to complete the list of 92, to conform to the so-called Periodic Table, there are yet seven elements to be found by your scientists. On Mars the most elementary school pupil is well informed on the subject, and has knowledge of the complete list among the new elements yet to be discovered by your chemists, and which exist in appreciable quantities on your Earth, is one which has the peculiar property of neutralizing Gravity.

This neutralizing is accomplished by screening off the gravitational pull when interposed between the Earth and the matter sought to be made immune from the attraction, just as you would insulate against the flow of electricity by inter- posing a non-conductor between two conducting metals.

The knowledge and use of this element on Mars has been utilized in the solution of our transportation problem. Instead of cumbersome railroads consuming energy at a great loss, we use an almost perfect flying or floating ship. It is made buoyant by being screened from the gravitational pull of the planet. [3]

[3] In the February issue of the "Electrical Experimenter, " (1920) which was published about a month after this information was received by revelation, the following article appeared—another startling confirmation of the truth contained herein, and points to the possibility that whatever is possible on one planet, is also possible on another, depending upon that planet's type of civilization and real knowledge, not superficial theory:

"Recently a cable dispatch from Rome brought the announcement that Prof. Maiorana discovered that lead balls swimming on a pool of mercury lost a certain amount of weight. It was explained that the weight was lost due to a screening effect which the mercury produced on the lead balls. In other words, mercury acts as a sort of insulator against the earth's gravitational waves. For gravitation certainly is propagated the same as other forms of energy, i.e., in wave form. Prof. T. J. See, famous investigator of Mare Island, California, in an address before the California Academy of Sciences, announced recently that his researches on gravitation in 1917 and his latest researches on molecular forces confirmed Maiorana's claim that the screening of gravitation has been shown to exist. In 1917, says Professor See, 'I explained the fluctuation of the Moon's main motion by the circular refraction of the sun's gravitation waves, as they are propagated through the solid body of our earth at the time of lunar eclipses. '

" 'I found also from dealings with capillary forces that quicksilver is indeed very resistant to the waves which produce molecular action, and this developed a new theory of the depression of the mercury in capillary tubes. This would tend to confirm Maiorana's claim that a basin of mercury beneath a suspended mass of lead may decrease the gravitation of the lead by a small amount. My researches on ether show conclusively that gravitation is due to waves in the ether, and

The Planet Mars and Its Inhabitants

certain very resistant bodies in the line of action may thus introduce a slight screening effect.'

"This reasoning opens up new avenues of thought of what may be accomplished in the future when we have found a perfect screen against gravitation."

Another subject of importance, that takes no little time to understand by the Martian student is the part played by the planet's satellites in the generation of Electro-Magnetic energy. The sun together with its circulating family of planets is a huge Electric motor, so a planet and its satellites are minor generators of Electric energy. Satellites have a higher importance and necessity than the mere creation of moonshine.

All the planets have their satellites, although your astronomers have not yet discovered any in the case of Mercury and Venus. The latter planet has a satellite whose distance is so close to its primary that its presence is lost in the intense reflection of light caused by Venus' cloudy atmosphere, which is much denser than that of your Earth. In the case of Mercury, owing to its extremely close proximity to the sun, its satellite probably never will be seen by observers on your Earth, as it is lost in the intense brilliance cast by the Solar Orb on this planet.

CHAPTER XII.

EDUCATION AND TRAINING OF THE INDIVIDUAL, VOCATIONAL DETERMINATION, SCHOOL AGE, MARRIAGE AND SCIENCE (Continued)

Everyone goes to school until the age of 16, that is, the length of time on Mars would correspond to 32 years on your Earth. The Martian year is nearly twice as long as on your globe.

There are many universities on Mars where students enter direct from their homes, where the primary and preparatory education is first inculcated in their minds. Wonderful teachers have charge of the students, and many truths not yet known on your Earth are taught. Special and particular attention is given to the subject of the development of Spiritual gifts to the end that all may come into man's Divine Heritage, the PEACE, POWER AND PLENTY of the KINGDOM OF GOD.

Each student is selected for his or her proper vocation, and this vocation is determined scientifically and accurately, for what benefits the individual also benefits the entire community.

Each individual is trained to perform his part in a manner that will ensure the unity and harmony of the entire industrial system of the planet, and each unit understands the dignity and importance of his position, no matter what that position may be, for on Mars no activity of human endeavor is considered menial; no one position in life is less important than the rest: all is God's work.

And so each gravitates to his special liking in the realm of physical activity, for God has created each individual for some particular work. Six hours is a day's work, the remainder of the time is devoted to recreation, music, lectures, and those general activities that best develop the highest spiritualities with the individual. For the Martians realize that life on the material plane is but temporary the isolation of the individual Divine Spark from the Infinite whole to the end that the personality may become for all Eternity self-conscious and in harmony with God, which means the inheritance of God's Kingdom for all time.

The Planet Mars and Its Inhabitants

Failure to come into harmony with God is destruction of the individuality, but not of the Divine in man, for that is indestructible: it always was and always will be.

Education on Mars is inculcated with a view principally of developing the individual spiritually in order to prepare one for the spiritual progress after the completion of the material probationary period as well as having life in greatest abundance during that period, and with this main end in view the subject of marriage, the rearing of children, receives special consideration and attention.

The pivotal idea is that when the time for mating arrives the selection of a wife by the prospective husband must be in accordance with true conjugal harmony, and this is not possible in the absence of Spiritual development. Hence, divorces are unknown with us, and to that end is special care taken in the matter of teaching the truth concerning the marital relation, the rearing of children and their Spiritual growth.

The marriage age for both sexes is about 35 years, in terms of your time measurements. The result of this early training is that the young couple just embarked on the "Sea of Matrimony, " are true mates and go through life without the usual occurrence of domestic turmoil so characteristic of your Earth's people.

Marriage on your Earth, with but few exceptions, has degenerated from God's holiest of institutions to a happy convenience for the gratification of the animal passions; and the rearing of children is an accident rather than a preconceived reality. Such marriages are unholy and destructive, and unless your people respond to a Spiritual awakening such as God's workers are now trying to inaugurate on your Earth the growing degeneracy will be augmented rather than diminished and the extinction of the race will be inevitable.

The curriculum of our schools embraces all branches of Domestic Science, as well as all the sciences, with the difference from your system that Spiritual development must be the principal task of those having supervision over the studies of the young.

One of the subdivisions of Domestic Science receiving particular attention on Mars is the PREPARATION OF FOODS. With an atmospheric pressure of only eight pounds to the square inch, water

The Planet Mars and Its Inhabitants

boils at 175 degrees on our planet. This temperature is inadequate for cooking foods properly, especially the coarser varieties. But recourse is had to the cooking of food in vacuum or under pressure, as the exigencies of the occasion demand.

Electrical energy is used most generally for producing heat, and the variety of foods, both animal and vegetal, are as extensive as on your planet, for the flora and fauna of Mars differs little from yours.

Martians are not excessive eaters, as their bodies do not require the gross foods so characteristic of your Earth. There are two reasons for this. In the first place the difference in the gravitational pull on Mars being thirty-eight one-hundredths to that of your Earth, obviates the necessity of supplying as much fuel to the human body as your physical make-up demands. In the second place the Martians partake of food to keep the body alive, and not for the vulgar pleasure afforded by the consumption of victuals. We eat to live: whereas most of your Earth tenants live to eat.

Although each individual has his particular place in the universe where he will excel in some kind of activity, there being no two persons in all Creation exactly alike, the student on Mars is given an opportunity to obtain a broad and comprehensive knowledge relating to all subjects, both material and spiritual.

The study of matter, divided as it is into a number of elements, offers an interesting field for study and research work, as does also its concomitant Cosmic Energy.

Compared to your Earth, industry on Mars, by the aid of labor-saving devices is perfect: and as a consequence the use of energy is considerable, especially so in the realm of Synthetic Chemistry. But it must be understood that the individual is taught that dependence must be placed rather on one's own dexterity, born of that God-given faculty of Intuition, than on the perfectness of a man-made machine, the creation of finite mind.

For it has so happened to races on other planets that complete degeneration and final extinction has come about by the entire dependence of the individual and afterwards of the entire race, on machinery to do the work required of the individual by the Creator, such dependence finally terminating in almost complete atrophy of the worker's intuitional faculties.

The Planet Mars and Its Inhabitants

This calamity will surely overtake your future generations if a halt is not called on the over-zealous adoption of automatic machines for most every line of industrial activity. You are now getting to the stage where the most simple and elementary mathematical problems are solved by merely pressing a few buttons or turning a crank, the operator understanding little or nothing of the fundamentals underlying the solution of the problems in hand. This means, in the near future, brain atrophy through disuse.

And so with other lines of industrial activity. Not one among a thousand workers engaged in making shoes can do other than make a heel or perform some simple operation, one of hundreds of units in the completion of a pair of shoes. And perhaps it would be impossible to find one individual whose intuitional faculties were developed to the extent that he could turn out the perfect, completed article.

In order to explain how far we have succeeded on Mars in harnessing a mighty universal force to the end of utilizing the same in turning our factory wheels, lighting our domiciles and giving warmth to our homes in winter, it might not be amiss to state a few facts concerning our knowledge of matter and energy.

We have learned that material life simply amounts to functioning in an Effect world. The Cause world is the Reality which is invisible to all while hampered with a physical body; that all forms of matter are but the manifestation of the same ultimate Essence; that this Essence is but a Divine Impulse—a thrust, as it were, in the Ether. That although we observe with our sensory organs many different kinds of matter, consisting of elements and compounds of elements: if we were able to resolve any of the different forms of matter before us into their ultimate units, these ultimate particles would all turn out to be the same thing, the "Divine Impulses" just mentioned.

Now you can best grasp the idea by imagining yourselves immersed in an Infinite sea of such Divine Impulses, just as a fish is immersed in an ocean of water. Everywhere. all about us, is a teeming maelstrom of motion. There is not a cubic centimeter of space that you can call at rest. All is eternal motion. All is Energy.

And out of this inexhaustible Cosmic Reservoir do we Martians draw our energy. And as the Divine Impulse is the ultimate essence of all matter and all energy, therefore you might imagine matter in its different aspects as Electrical in origin. As Electricity is a manifestation of the Divine Impulse, then the only Reality in the Universe is GOD.

We have learned to utilize this Cosmic Energy by getting into harmony with its origin—GOD—for only through God can true knowledge be obtained.

On your Earth you have devised a very crude method for utilizing Electrical Energy. You expend more energy by burning coal or using water power than you derive from your electrical pump: for a dynamo is nothing more than a pump. Your machines do not generate electrical power for, as stated before you are immersed in an Infinite sea of energy.

On Mars we have learned to draw directly on this Infinite reservoir of energy. We have learned the law as you some day must.

Located at convenient points on our planet are high towers, capped with suitable receiving apparatus. In turn this energy is transmitted to different parts of our globe where it is used. We do not require wires to transmit energy. Our landscape is neither disfigured with unsightly wires, nor is it covered with a pall of black smoke. We devised a more perfect method of power production and transmission.

The relativity of time, space, motion and matter is an actuality brought to the attention of advanced students on Mars. An understanding of this truth exemplifies the unreality of the world of gross matter and the importance of gaining knowledge concerning Spiritual truths; for the latter are the only real tangible treasures worthy of one's efforts in their acquisition. Already a knowledge of these truths is beginning to be sought for by some of the more spiritually enlightened inhabitants of your Earth; but so immersed in the unreal things of life is the vast majority of your Earth people that it will take a long time before the present seed-sowing toward this end will bear fruit.

The seed-sowing referred to is the work of enlightenment now going on by a mighty group of Spiritual intelligences who, at the present day, have in hand the task of Spiritual reformation on your Earth. Only Truth can stand in the end. All that is unreal or false must ultimately give way to truth, and Omniscience has willed that the day when error shall be no more shall be hastened.

There are other planes of existence for the Spirit: many of them.

But they are simply extensions beyond your limited vision; for as long as you function in a world of unreality and error your Spiritual vision is incapable of discerning what lies beyond your present horizon, and must remain dormant. Material eyes are but the windows of the Soul, and your environment has so beclouded your vision that you grasp but little of the real things beyond.

CHAPTER XIII.

MUSIC AN EXPRESSION OF THE FATHER

All material expressions of the Father, from the simplest chemical element to the most complex compound; from the one-celled protoplasmic life germ to the most complex organism, are Vibratory in their ultimate nature.

As has been stated elsewhere in this book, material life is the vibratory reflection from the Cause world into an Effect world. The universe is a vibratory expression of an absolute Reality—GOD: a material expression of Divine Harmony. And as Harmony is an expression of the Father, its antithesis, Discord, is the creation of man.

Of all the vibrations that more fully express the Father and arouse the Emotional within the soul, Music must of necessity head the list.

Owing to man's degeneration or fall, on your Earth, he has lost all receptibility to the more refined vibratory tones of the chromatic scale.

And for the same reason he has lost receptibility to intermediate vibrations in the COLOR spectrum, which has clouded or stultified his visional faculties. The long waves of the Infra-red and the short waves of the Ultra-violet ends of the spectrum are invisible to your Earth people except in rare cases of developed mediumship, though your photograph plates are somewhat sensitive to these vibrations.

You are immersed in commercialism and other selfish pursuits while all around you is a beautiful RAINBOW UNIVERSE, vibrating with music too heavenly for your dulled perceptions to enjoy.

On Mars the development of the Musical talent is held to be of primary importance. The laws of Harmony are part of the curriculum of all schools, and all necessary paraphernalia for its proper exposition are provided. We have instruments for measuring tone vibrations of so delicate a pitch that the existence of these tones would be a blank to the gross material ears of the inhabitants of your world.

The Planet Mars and Its Inhabitants

Music arouses the innermost emotions of the soul and its effect on the individual is proportionate to his degree of spiritual development. Music is harmony, but it also creates an atmosphere of harmony.

The music of the spheres is a living reality, for Harmony is the very essence of the Cosmos. By Music of the Spheres is meant the harmonious interrelation of all spiritual planes. Every unit in the universe is in perfect accord one with the other, and all are functioning in perfect unison. Every Solar Orb and every Planet responds to Harmonious law. The Cosmos as a whole is the expression of a Divine Symphony.

When man's spiritual progress has attained a degree of enfoldment entitling him to come into possession of his Divine Heritage then will the sublime vibrations of the spheres be a reality to him.

On Mars divers instruments are used for producing musical harmony, and much of this harmony is of such a subtle nature that your crude instruments could not give expression to it.

We have a means of producing harmony of the highest order by utilizing Ethereal Electric Vibration which produces light vibrations corresponding to tone production. for true Electric Vibration is real music. This device resembles a series of globes. all transparent, colorless when not in action. But immediately they are allowed to produce music they become units of color and tone work that would give you the impression of SEEING AND HEARING A RAINBOW SIMULTANEOUSLY. You are not ready to receive the scientific explanation of this phenomenon, but we are ready to give it to you at any time.

Singing is also highly developed on our planet, for it is the first expression of harmony that the child is taught. This is true for the reason that vocal music is the most natural expression of harmonious vibrations. Much time is devoted to ensemble work among our people of all ages. This chorus work is of great benefit to all partaking, for individually and collectively much inspiration is received; and the tremendous Love-force loosened by this united expression of harmony becomes a phenomenal power and stimulus—a purifying agent for soul and body. This will help you to realize why disease is unknown to us.

The Planet Mars and Its Inhabitants

In the development of the musical talents of the individual on Mars the pupil is impressed with the necessity of expressing the true self, and the original improvisation or composition is the method by which the pupil expresses his understanding of the subject. No one attempts to ape the technique or genius of another, for on Mars all are geniuses. This is true in every form of activity. All must be creators to express individuality.

When an individual on Mars has surpassed all others in some special expression of Divine Harmony the product of his genius is for the benefit of all, hence copyrights and patents are unknown on our planet.

The Planet Mars and Its Inhabitants

CHAPTER XIV

AERONAUTICS, INHABITED PLANETS, SECTARIANISM

A great deal of interest is being manifested in your city this morning (April 25, 1920), over the Aeronautical Show. You imagine the Flying machines wonderful mechanisms; but in their present state they will not lift you out of your atmosphere. You have yet to perfect a real airship.

Your Flying machines are cumbersome and awkward, and they consume lots of fuel and make a deal of noise. It can hardly be said they are harmonious with the music of the spheres, but then it is only a sample of your Earth's development.

You have seen the seagulls soar over the water seemingly without motion; and yet they go up and down, turning this way and that without effort. This is the best idea I can give you of our airships, which really soar. No sound, no discordant vibrations disturb the quiet of the Martian atmosphere, and the tranquility of the Mars people.

When you have learned the secret of how to tap the Universal Reservoir of Cosmic Power, then will you evolve a perfect Flying machine such as we have. A great deal of interest is also being centered on an attempt to signal Mars, and your apparatus is not fine enough to receive our waves. But success will come to you in another decade, and we will be able to get something through for your scientific world.

It is gratifying to know that a large portion of your population entertain the belief that Mars is inhabited: and also that the possibilities point to the fact that other planets are inhabited.

You have advanced a long way to come to that belief, but you are yet a long way from the truth. You are on the eve of an awakening and much will come through the discoveries of scientists who are devoting their lives to the study of Truth. It is true that only a few of that number are bold enough to proclaim all they discover. and they must bear the brunt of much harsh criticism. In the end, however, ignorance must give way to Light.

We look upon your inventions with much amusement, and yet with great interest, just as you would look upon your children's finest toys. We are much older than you and are doing all we can to help your scientists by impressing them with thoughts that will lead them to discover new truths, and our interest never flags. How could it if we are doing the Father's work? For it is the Father's great pleasure to give His children all they can receive.

If you could cut loose from your world conventions and could perceive new ideas; if you would but disregard man-made theories and open your minds and souls to the Father's Revelations, it would not be long before your sin-cursed and forsaken Earth would be changed into a Paradise.

But the tendency among you if to think as your forefathers thought rather than cut new paths. However, your children of this generation are of a different sort, and they must be taught the importance of DEVELOPING THE SPIRITUAL INTELLECT. There is MORE INDIVIDUALISM being born into the world today than ever before. THERE ARE FEWER CHILDREN, BUT THEY ARE STRONGER (the year 1920).

THESE CHILDREN, WITH THEIR ORIGINALITY AND ESOTERIC TENDENCIES WILL BRING ON A REVOLUTION ON YOUR PLANET THAT WILL END BY DESTROYING YOUR THREADBARE DOGMATISM. This tendency is evidenced by the recent failure of the Interchurch movement. It has been the habit on your planet that you cannot accomplish anything without raising immense sums of money,

It is not money that does the real work but rather PERSONAL SERVICE. People are inclined to give almost everything than personal service. If each person lived the Christ Life there would be no need of money. A close study of the Mars Economic system will demonstrate that truth.

CHAPTER XV.

LIFE AN ATTRIBUTE OF THE ENTIRE UNIVERSE. THE PLANET JUPITER

LIFE IS AN ATTRIBUTE OF THE ENTIRE UNIVERSE. Go forth on a moonless night and behold the firmament emblazoned with its myriad of scintillating stars, solar orbs, nebulae, world-systems in the making: the galactic circle, a jeweled band athwart the canopy of Heaven; a seething maelstrom of Light: countless suns in space all expressing the one reality, OMNISCIENCE.

Only presumptuous man can question the Divine Intent in the creation of the Infinite number of giant suns, stupendous worldwide systems, and place his particular world-unit at the center of the Cosmos.

Man contemplates this handiwork of God as a mere adjunct (more ornamental than useful) to his terrestrial environment, conceitedly thinking that the Father's only consideration is centered about himself.

As these life-giving orbs are countless in number, their orbits extending as they do to Infinity in all directions, so is it with the habitable worlds in space. Some there are where life is not yet possible: worlds not yet far removed from their primitive state: not long since condensed from fire mist: others where life has just begun: others on whose surfaces live teeming millions of God's creatures, just as you live and others have lived before you. And there are other worlds whose life-cycle has been run; where intelligent life has ceased: where world-disintegration has set in. For this is in accordance with the universal law of Growth and Decay—a law that exempts neither the one-celled amoeba, nor the complex Solar system whirling yonder in Infinite space.

For all that comes from the Father into material expression must some day revert to its primordial state.

You have thus far received much concerning the idealistic conditions on Mars, whose planetary career is now reaching the zenith of its Cosmic cycle, and whose denizens have progressed to a degree of Divine unfoldment not yet attained by many worlds.

The Planet Mars and Its Inhabitants

It is necessary that you now receive some information relating to one of the less-advanced planets belonging to the family of our sun, in order you may be able to learn by contrast something of the wonders of God's work.

JUPITER, owing to its prodigious size, being nearly eleven times larger than your Earth, but whose density is proportionately less, might well be styled the Master Planet of our system.

Jupiter is well blessed with satellites, having eight, a description of which is not necessary at this time. This planet is in what might be styled its primary evolutionary stage where life has just begun. This life has not evolved beyond the unicellular, or amoebic stage; and it will be only after the lapse of a long period of time, measured in Geological units, when more complex organisms will appear: and many of these periods will come and go before this planet's surface will have attained a proper development for the propagation of intelligences capable of being classed with the denizens of your Earth.

Long before that age arrives Jupiter's surface and atmosphere will undergo a tremendous change. Mighty planetary cataclysms will raise new mountain ranges; new continents will appear, and the present land surfaces on this planet will sink, to be covered with slime and water, to rise again in the centuries to come, for the Father's love and solicitude will provide, as it has in the case of all His Celestial Creations, a bountiful supply of stored-up radiant energy, such as coal and petroleum, and other elements, for the comfort of those who will inhabit this giant among the worlds of this system in time to come.

Jupiter still retains much of its internal heat, which gives this planet a very high mean temperature. Its atmosphere is still very dense, and owing to the very rapid evaporation of water due to the extreme heat a constant cloud canopy covers its surface, which only dissipates occasionally in a slight degree, at which times only the sun penetrates to the surface of the globe. By reason of the constant thick cloud canopy over the surface of Jupiter the planet is enveloped in deep gloom and darkness. As radiation is arrested to a marked degree by the clouds and atmosphere the temperature is very humid as well as hot. In this steam environment grow forests of fern and fungus-like trees and rank vegetal growths which will in the course of time be preserved as coal for the races destined to inhabit this planet. This vegetal growth is a flora that knows not bloom or seed, but is propagated by root and spores, a flora most primitive in type, but which will in time evolve through the law of mutation and adaptation into a diversified and useful vegetal kingdom for the races yet to come on the planet.

Owing to the tremendous gravitational pull on Jupiter present organisms are, and future ones will be evolved along specially modified lines, in order that they may encompass the least possible volume, just as the denizens of the extreme depths of your oceans have evolved. The modification is necessary that organisms mat be able to function on a planet where the difference in gravity is as one to three compared with your Earth. In other words a minimum density is necessary to produce maximum lightness.

As there is no lesser or greater in the economy of Nature (Nature is God Manifest), the most infinitesimal mote in the universe is as perfect within itself as is the most gigantic sun. Size is but relative. The anatomy of the midget is as perfect and complex as is that of the mammoth, and so there exist in the universe inhabited worlds that are relatively very small.

Circulating around the sun in orbits between Mars and Jupiter are numerous small planets or asteroids. One in particular, which is known to your astronomers as Vesta, is encompassed by an atmosphere and is inhabited by diminutive people and a correspondingly diminutive fauna and flora. The diameter of Vesta is about 500 miles, although your astronomers give its size, erroneously, as much smaller.

While the subject of these discourses is mainly Spiritual you are getting many scientific facts, and although not a volume of them you are getting a proper understanding of the Cosmos.

The universe with all its suns and planets is analogous to a perfect watch. Each sun and planet moves over a prescribed orbit in a given time mathematically proportional to the movements of all the other celestial bodies, just as the geared wheels of the watch conform to their prescribed movements. The celestial bodies are seemingly actuated by invisible gears and are held rigidly in their proper places by a mighty force whose power is incalculable. This is evidenced by the fact that all celestial bodies conform to that inexorable law, Divine Harmony.

The Planet Mars and Its Inhabitants

That all planets describe equal areas in the same time in their ceaseless journeyings, and that the square of the time of their periods is as the cube of their distance from their common centers, is an exemplification of the reign of God's harmonious laws.

You must remember that Empirical knowledge is but a perverted view of Truth. All the fleeting things of life are but dross: their apparent reality an illusion. Material life is but a projection from the Cause world into the Effect world. Man is but a reflection of a reality that transcends his material vision.

You are on the threshold of a great awakening on your planet, which is yet in great darkness, but the dawn of a better day is nigh. Christ is coming into His Kingdom, which must be in the hearts of the people. His Second Coming means that He will come into your lives with the Power of the Spirit. This can only become possible through an awakened understanding of Spiritual laws. Although man on your Earth is in great darkness it is not the darkness of Jupiter, which planet must undergo many changes before it reaches your evolutionary stage.

COMMUNICATION BETWEEN PLANETS in our system and your Earth will be realized in a short time, and the INITIAL MESSAGE WILL BE FROM MARS. This event will herald A NEW ERA for the people of your Earth, for it will be an important factor in the BREAKING DOWN OF THE MEDIEVAL DOGMATISM of the past, A NARROW-MINDED THEOLOGY built upon a perverted corruption of God's limitless universe: a universe narrowed down to your Earth and the inhabitants thereof.

Man's presumptuousness and sophistry is in direct ratio to his ignorance, and that is one reason why materialism holds sway among a majority of your so-called learned scientists and the people generally. But the materialism of the masses is not so degenerating and destructive as the impossible dogmas entertained by your numerous sects WHO HAVE MADE GOD, WHO IS INFINITE LOVE, AN ANTHROPOMORPHIC MONSTER. These dogmas are priestly inventions created to frighten God's children; to make of man, created after the image of God a crawling, servile creature, instead of what he really should be, the highest manifestation of the Divine, the culmination of God's handiwork.

CHAPTER XVI

THE RISEN CHRIST Easter Sunday, April 4, 1920

Your Earth's inhabitants are celebrating today the Resurrection of your Savior—by gratifying the desires of Self.

We of Mars do not have such events to commemorate for we never crucified Him. We opened the door to His wonderful Truth.

Not one of your Earth's inhabitants can perform the miracles Christ did, but we can. Our leaders, who are our advisers, guides and Spiritual teachers are Christlike men who can do all the works that Christ and His disciples did. He said. "These signs do follow them that believe, " and we have never stopped believing.

Your condition is pitiful. There is nothing but darkness between you and the Truth Christ tried to give you. Christ is only an idea on your planet and not a reality in the hearts of your people. Their whole thought, for weeks past, has been devoted to their personal adornment, and in preparing festivals for this occasion.

In your churches, where they seem to observe the period of Christ's suffering, it is only a form. They go through their vain repetition of prayers, that have no soul in them, and your six weeks of so-called Lent is only a mockery of its real significance.

If you would live the Christ life you would not crucify Him daily in the flesh, but would come to that consciousness that He is risen in your soul. You are continually crucifying Christ all over your planet in the same way that you crucified Jesus Christ, for you either deny Him or pervert His Truth to suit your selfishness.

All of the people on Mars have lived on other planets before, except your Earth. The Earth has not advanced enough to be placed in the line of progression yet. However, the time is near when you will experience that progression. It will be after you are high enough spiritually to receive word from the Martians through mediums. This work evidences the fact that you are beginning that experience now. Take hope, for after the obscure darkness must come the dawn.

The Planet Mars and Its Inhabitants

Your whole Earth is now in terrible travail, but the result will be the birth of the new Christ Spirit.

You get glimpses now and then of the real Christ Life, but do you, or can you realize what life on a planet is like when all the inhabitants live the Christ Life every day? That is why we have the wonderful manifestations of the Father's Love in our intricate and delicate mechanisms, and in our utilization of Cosmic Energy. It is thus that we receive the Father's wondrous gifts. But Mars never became what it is until God purified it by His Son's example, and we accepted Him as our Savior WITHOUT MURDER. Your planet damned itself to many bloody aeons by the rejection of Him, and your Religion has been blood, blood, blood! In your last five years you have been given enough blood to drown all the martyrs you have given to your bloody god.

Your planet is in slavery. You are slaves to your conventionalities. They are like shackles on your souls: like bands of iron. And yet you cling to them until it seems you do not want freedom.

It is only Truth that will free you; and as long as you cling to false ideals and sham systems you must expect to be slaves.

Pin your faith not in material money, but in Spiritual Wealth. "Take no heed of the morrow. " Be of good cheer. MAKE WIDE THE OPENING TO THE SPIRIT! HE WILL ENTER!

CHAPTER XVII.

PHYSICAL ENVIRONMENT THE RESULT OF SPIRITUAL CAUSES

"For they have sown the wind
and they shall reap the whirlwind." (Hosea, 8:7)

The Creator and Dominator of the entire Universe is DIVINE MENTALITY.

The only real actuality that confronts sentient beings is MIND. We are born, live and have our being amidst physical surroundings that in final analysis are mere illusions. This idea is not new.

It forms the base of most systems of philosophy from the dawn of civilization to the present day.

Our physical environment is the result of our mental attitude. Mars is blessed with a climatic tranquility that would surpass the understanding of an Earth dweller. But this was not always so.

In proportion to the spiritual unfoldment of the inhabitants of a planet so is the degree of climatic tranquility enjoyed by them. This may, at first reading, appear far-fetched, but it is true nevertheless.

Those who live on a material plane are immersed in the Effect world. The dominating and primary influence that gives rise to all material phenomena have their inception in the Cause world—the world of Spirit. Hence the turbulence of the elements originate, through the law of Vibration, deep down in the mentalities of those who make up the population of a planet. Cloudbursts, severe wind storms and other disturbances of Nature are all adjuncts of the spirit of war and rapine.

When a race has discarded the pursuit of false ideals and comes into harmony with the Father then there occurs a corresponding change in its physical environment by reason of the vibratory influences at work. These influences have their inception in the mentalities of sentient beings who are doing the Father's work in the advancement of the races of men throughout the entire physical universe.

The Planet Mars and Its Inhabitants

This same vibratory law is at work throughout all physical planes, and a knowledge of this law was referred to by Christ when He said: "THE KINGDOM OF GOD IS WITHIN YOU."

On Mars, owing to the high spiritual state of its inhabitants, who are in harmony with their Creator, climatic conditions are, compared with your world, most perfect. However, there was a time, measured in terms of your millions of years, when the elements on Mars were as agitated and capricious as they are today on your blood-stained globe. That was before man on Mars had enfolded spiritually,

As the Martians progressed and unfolded spiritually there occurred a subsidence in the roughness of the elements: and today our planet is blessed with a tranquility proportionate to the high Mental state of its inhabitants.

CHAPTER XVIII.

MATERIAL LIFE A LESSON

At the expense of what may appear as painful reiteration it is my desire to impress upon the readers of this book this Truth: Material life is necessary to unfold character, to develop the real self, the Divine part in man: the only principle that endures forever.

There is a lesson in every phase of work, in every joy, in every sorrow. That lesson is LOVE. Until you have fully realized this truth you will not become full heirs in the Kingdom of God. "He that loveth is born of God."

Christ taught that the Kingdom was not of your Earth, and that all material things are transitory and would ultimately vanish like mist.

The story of Mars is a lesson to you as to what may be accomplished towards a more harmonious relation with the Father: towards a truer realization of God's real Kingdom. But in any event you should not idolize the Mars people, for the Father's Kingdom is more perfect. Mars' idealism is only a degree in the progress in the Cosmic Family of worlds. The soul must really strive for a higher goal.

The Martians, after ages of time, have mastered their natural passions in suppressing self, but they have other heights to scale. But he who conquers a sordid environment; he who rises from a black pool of iniquity; he who finds the Father's Kingdom amidst an uncompromising warfare with sin deserves more credit than he who is favored by circumstances of birth with more congenial surroundings and a higher Spiritual environment.

You must remember that the individual on Mars, although living amidst an idealism, is beset with problems of life also. Our problems are more subtle and of a very different character than you are accustomed to deal with. Every plane of life has its complexities. If this were not so, the stimulus for growth would be weak indeed. Your most apparent problems are material only to your understanding, since you are living under a most pernicious social and economic system, a system which puts a premium on selfishness.

All sentient entities are functioning in a universe of Relativity, and the perfectness of the Martian character and the ideal material and spiritual aspects of the planet are so by comparison only.

Martians are self-conscious of their shortcomings and aspire to higher things in God's Kingdom, for progress is eternal and the ultimate goal is never reached on the material plane of action, for the pinnacle of all progress is God. "BE YE PERFECT, EVEN AS YOUR FATHER IN HEAVEN IS ALSO PERFECT."

CHAPTER XIX.

A MARTIAN HOME

The HOME is the moulder of Character in the individual, and in most cases the Home influences determine the future of the man.

Home influences are the most lasting and abide by the individual unto the end of his material career.

All the habitations of the people of Mars are beautiful, and a brief description of one will give our reader an understanding of the other millions of homes on the planet.

I will take you into a Martian home in the city of Urid the Beautiful. The rooms are large and commodious. Sunlight, which has been filtered through translucent glass to temper and rob it of its glare, floods every room.

There are no stairs to climb, for the five or six rooms—depending on the size of the family—form a rectangle with a court in the center. There is a fountain in the center of the court, and beautiful flowers grow in profusion. Birds of vivid plumage fill the air with their song.

In one of the large rooms a mother sits at a sewing machine making a garment. For the Martians use these machines too, although they are a great improvement on yours. Not all the clothing is made in the homes, but much of it is, and this is easily understood when you recall that the Martians are true artists and possessed of great originality.

The mother's attention is now and then centered on a very small child who sits on a velvety carpet. This carpet would be a most wonderful acquisition in the home of a man of wealth on your Earth. It has a soft, fluffy pile two inches thick, and makes a most comfortable floor for the baby to play upon. This baby is about 18 months old, and plays with toys just as your Earth babies do.

A beautiful young girl enters the room. She is dressed in a simple becoming gown of white, and she carries her school books with her. After removing her hat and putting her books away she begins to tell her mother of the wonderful things learned at school that day. She is studying the Harmony of Music, particularly the relationship between Electro-Magnetic Vibrations and Music.

The mother shows much interest, and from her store of knowledge clears up many doubtful points in the mind of her daughter. And so the hours pass quickly until the father comes home and joins the family circle.

The walls of the room are white, and are relieved here and there by the most beautiful tapestries. The few furnishings of the room express beauty through the artistry that is born of Love.

There is a lack of useless furniture and bric-a-brac in the room.

A table, a few chairs and a receptacle for books, also a couch, complete the furnishings. But this simplicity in the matter of furniture adds a spirit of freedom to the home.

There is no kitchen drudgery in store for the Housewife. The family repair to a dining-room where food is served by the mother. The food has just arrived from a central depot in a mechanical contrivance which runs underground. After the meal has been partaken of, the soiled dishes are returned in the same manner by which they were conveyed to the home.

Later in the evening the family prepares to attend a lecture or musical concert nearby. Or perhaps a visit to some distant part is considered, in which case an airship is ordered from a public aerodrome.

CHAPTER XX.

ART

As Harmony is an expression of the Father, its coexistent, Art, is an expression of the laws of Rhythm through the individual when permanently registered in a material way.

The more a created object conforms to the laws of Harmony the more pleasing it is to the eye.

The artist gives expression to his soul within with paint brush, chisel or loom, and the quality of his production is proportionate to the development of his spiritual nature.

All of God's creatures are artists, although only a small percentage of His evolutionary creatures are able to express materially what lies hidden in the soul. Hence, a beautifully executed painting, statue or tapestry appeals to and interests almost everyone, even though few are able to execute their own artistic impressions.

The reason for this is that the average physical makeup is defective and therefore affords a poor vehicle for the expression of the real entity. Then again, artistic ability is a question of individual development.

Primordial man's efforts to depict that which delighted his soul were crude indeed, compared with the creations of your world's foremost artists today. But in a relative sense only, for the state of your art is as far behind the art of the Martians as are the carvings of your prehistoric cavemen behind the productions of your Michael Angelos. As man unfolds spiritually there is a corresponding advance in his artistic point of view.

This is evidenced by the fact that art has flourished more on your Earth among those races and individuals who are spiritually inclined. The products of the monastery and cloister in the Middle Ages are witness to this fact.

Amongst a materially inclined people whose selfish instincts have stultified their souls; a people whose ultimate goal is the acquisition of material things; a people whose only ambition is to satisfy self: a people whose ideas of real happiness are the pursuit of material pleasures, art has little place except as a fad.

This is the condition today in many parts of your world, and especially so on your Western continent. Prize fights and the sensualities of the stage interest many more people than do Art galleries and the beauties of Nature.

The fact that God is the Supreme Artist of the Universe can be established not only with the microscope, but with one's natural eyes. Divine Art is expressed in every atom comprising the universe; and poor indeed is he in Spiritual gifts who fails to feast his eyes on God's handiwork.

As Art is an expression of God's law of Harmony it can be said that its development on Mars has been a stimulus to the development of every line of planetary activity and enters into every phase of Martian social and industrial system.

As every one of God's creatures is an artist in the making, every Martian is a developed artist. Hence, every product of the loom or forge on our planet is an artistic production, and reflects in a material way the soul of the creator.

The incentive before the Martian is to work for the pleasure of working, which in ultimate analysis is God's work. Of course such a system of industrial activity would be impossible among a partially developed people.

Art on Mars typifies man's spiritual and material progress on this planet. This planet's past history and present achievements are woven into the products of the looms. The warp and woof of our beautiful tapestries, so much in evidence in every home, express the Spirituality of the Martian people; as do also the creations of the Martian sculptors, and the works of those who use brush and paint.

Some of the most beautiful productions of Mars art in painting, sculpture or tapestry depict the scenes and various episodes incident to Christ's visit to Mars 10,000 years ago. They show many wonderful works of the Master, but we do not call them Miracles for, as later art shows, the leaders of Martian spiritual attainment were and are true disciples and do also the works of the Master.

The Planet Mars and Its Inhabitants

Mars' past has been one of achievement spiritually, and naturally in a material way also, so when the Martian artist weaves the story of the past in his loom there are no misgivings, for the Martian past is not fraught with hate, sin and suffering.

CHAPTER XXI.

SCIENTIFIC SOPHISTRY

"For we are of yesterday, and know nothing, because our days upon Earth are a shadow."
Job 8:9.

The term "Scientific Sophistry" well fits your multitude of theories concerning Truth.

Science which connotes a higher wisdom of hidden things has degenerated on your Earth from its original purpose (the overthrow of ignorance and superstition and the development among intelligent beings of a near approximation of Ultimate Truth) to an orthodox dogmatism, which today is on a par with the unreality which this selfsame science has sought to eliminate from the shallowness of the human mind.

It is quite true that the modern scientific method of investigation: that is, along the lines of Observation, followed by the formation of a theory, and finally by demonstration, has resulted in the release of millions of souls from a darker thraldom than that which now besets them, but nevertheless, the human race on your planet now undergoing its probationary experience, is to be pitied for its blindness in matters of real import, namely SPIRITUAL TRUTHS.

Your scientific methods instead of leading you onward towards the Central Sun of Spiritual enlightenment has so beclouded your vision that your race today—that is, the so-called enlightened and learned portions of your population—have been deflected from the main path, and they will soon find themselves pursuing an illusionary will-o'-the-wisp.

Another result of the adoption of the modern scientific method has been the tendency of those endeavoring to bring light into the dark nooks and crannies of human existence, to immerse themselves in an abysmal materialism from which rescue is almost hopeless.

This condition is the result of a loss of Spiritual vision, and is the final effort on the part of scientists to explain the riddle of human existence in accordance with a cleverly thought out, but most amazingly deficient, mechanistic conception of life.

Since the inception of modern Science on your Earth, based on the scientific method of investigation, its devotees adopted a spirit of skepticism concerning all problems of human activity not susceptible to measurement with the foot-rule, or analysis with the test tube, with the result that the newer Science of Psychology was invented to supply a reasonable and material explanation for the subtle and mystifying phenomena of the human mind.

That the conceivers of this science of Psychology have been successful is attested by the many remarkable explanations given to account for everyday manifestations of human and animal mentality.

I will venture to say that this idea applies to all branches of modern science as there seems to be no class of phenomena in the entire universe, whether in the realm of chemistry, physics or psychology but what can be clearly elucidated to the satisfaction of all scientists with the aid of an adequate terminology. So, today your Science in final analysis, has degenerated into a system of clever word-juggling.

It is true there are today in the ranks of your foremost investigators and God-inspired men who are seeking Truth. Their names and their achievements will be treasured by a grateful posterity, and it is to be regretted that their declarations, based upon tireless investigation and honest opinion, are derided by their fellow-workers in the Realm of Truth.

All your scientific theories are based upon certain postulates that in time are out of agreement with observed facts, and you are compelled to cast those postulates aside, adopt others and theorize anew. This fruitless search for Truth must go on until a divergence is made from the blind trail and the right path is found that will lead you to the ultimate goal.

Be not surprised, then, that the revelations in this book will meet with the usual criticisms launched at every new idea of Truth that has been given to your world from the time man first walked erect and beheld the stars in the firmament of God. Error must and will dissolve presently in the presence of Truth, which will abide with you for all time. HELP HASTEN THE DAY OF THE LORD.